william Pra

Maisie in the Rainforest

For William! Hello from Aileen Paterson

Maisie in the Rainforest

Author and illustrator Aileen Paterson

This book is dedicated to Professor Sandy McIndoe.

Would you like to be a Super Cat? Many rainforests in the world are in danger. These organisations can give you advice about what children can do to help.

ROYAL BOTANIC GARDEN
Inverleith Row
Edinburgh
EH3 5LR

WORLD WILDLIFE FUND
Panda House
11-13 Ockford Road
Godalming, Surrey

FRIENDS OF THE EARTH
26-28 Underwood Street
London
N1 7JQ

EARTHLIFE
10 Belgrave Square
London
SW1X 8PH

Published in 1992 by
The Amaising Publishing House Ltd.
P.O. Box
Musselburgh
EH21 7UJ
Scotland

Telephone 031-665 8237

Printed and Bound by Scotprint Ltd, Musselburgh

Reprint Code 10 9 8 7 6 5 4 3 2 1

It is the publisher's policy to use paper
manufactured from sustainable forests.

Other Maisie Titles in the Series:

Maisie and the Space Invader

Maisie and the Posties

Maisie's Festival Adventure

Maisie goes to School

Maisie goes to Hospital

Maisie Loves Paris

What Maisie did Next

Maisie was flying down to Rio --- all by herself!

Granny had brought her down to London in the train and put her on board a jet plane at Heathrow Airport, and now she was off to South America to visit Daddy.

Maisie felt sad when it was time to say goodbye to Granny, but she cheered up when the plane took off. An air hostess looked after her and brought her a lovely lunch. Fried chicken, ice-cream and two milkshakes! The pilot showed her the controls which help to fly the plane. After that she watched a film starring her hero, *SUPER CAT.*

Maisie growled whenever the bad cats appeared, and purred when Super Cat flew in and fixed everything.

But the flight from London to Rio takes fourteen hours, which is a long time for a little kitten like Maisie to spend travelling. She likes running and jumping and, most of all, *talking*. She glanced hopefully at the stripey cat in the stripey suit sitting next to her, but he paid no attention. He was busy reading a pile of papers. Maisie peeped to see what was so interesting, but there were no pictures, just rows of numbers.

Maisie yawned. Her fluffy head drooped. Soon she fell fast asleep.

A few hours later, the stripey cat, still busy with his nose in his work, was suddenly startled by loud yeowlings nearby! WRROW! WRROW! MIAOUW! GRRROW!

He was even more startled when the kitten sitting next to him kicked all his papers up in the air and knocked his glasses off. "Hey!" he shouted. "What do you think you are doing?" Maisie opened her eyes and looked around her.

"Oh dear," she said, feeling very silly. "I'm SO sorry, I was dreaming I was Super Cat saving the world. I'll pick everything up right away." And so she did.

The stripey cat put the papers away in his briefcase and smiled at her.

"Thank you. Don't worry, there's no harm done. Allow me to introduce myself. I'm from New York. My name is Stanley Catnipp the Third, but everyone calls me S.C."

"Hello," said Maisie, shaking his paw. "My name is Maisie Mackenzie, the First. Everyone calls me Maisie, but sometimes Mrs McKitty from next door calls me a Purrfect Pest. She says Granny is too easy-osy with me. We live in Edinburgh . . . would you care for a piece of Edinburgh rock, Mr S.C.?"

"Thank you kindly, Maisie. My, this is lovely candy! Now, tell me all about yourself."

Maisie was delighted to have someone to talk to! She told him about her friends, and her Granny, and said she was on her way to meet her Daddy.

"We are going on a trip up the Amazon river! You see, my

Daddy is an explorer, and last week he sent me a telegram asking me to come and join him. There's a special forest he wants me to see. It's called a *rainforest*, and Daddy says it might disappear soon."

"My word," said her new friend, "A *disappearing* forest! It sounds very mysterious."

"I think it must be a magical place. Granny said it sounds very wet, so she packed my umbrella and wellyboots in case I get a chill. And I've got cream to keep the midgies away. We have champion midgies in Scotland. They can bite you right through your jersey! My friend Archie lent me his camera, and Mrs McKitty gave me a packet of porridge to keep my strength up. So I'm all ready for my expedition. Are you going on an expedition too?"

"I'm afraid not, Maisie. I wish I was . . . it sounds so exciting! I'm going to a meeting in Rio. It will be very boring."

He told Maisie that when he was a kitten, he too had wanted to be Super Cat and fly all over the world doing good. Now he did fly all over the world making millions of dollars, but he never seemed to have time to make friends or have fun. Maisie said it

was time he had a holiday, and that he must come to Scotland. He would have lots of fun there, playing football with her friends. Granny would teach him to say 'Och aye, the noo', and sing Scottish songs like 'I left my heart in Auchtermuchty'. Mr Catnipp laughed and said he would love to come and meet Maisie's Granny. He gave her his telephone number, and said they must keep in touch. When the plane landed, they waved goodbye. Mr Catnipp was dashing off to his meeting. A big black car was waiting for him.

And there was *Daddy*, waiting for MAISIE!

"Maisie!" he cried, picking her up for a cuddle. "It's *wonderful* to see you again, my wee tattie scone."

It was very hot in Rio! Maisie had to take off her woolly jersey and put on a T-shirt before they set off on the rest of their journey. They still had a long way to go!

First of all, Daddy flew them in his own plane over miles of jungle and mountains.

They landed on an airstrip beside the Amazon river, then went on board a steamship which carried them far upstream.

When they arrived at a little harbour by a village, they got out and all their luggage was put in a canoe. Daddy gave a special whistle, and from out of the jungle stepped a spotty cat. Daddy said he was his friend, and that his name was TOOCOOROOCOO.

Toocooroocoo paddled the canoe the rest of the way, up a small river, till at last they came to his home, the special rainforest Maisie had come so far to see.

It was dark by the time they arrived. Daddy carried Maisie up a rope ladder to his house high up in a tree. She was so tired she jumped right into bed --- but she fell right out again! Her bed was a hammock and Maisie took quite a while to get the hang of it, but at last she climbed in and fell asleep.

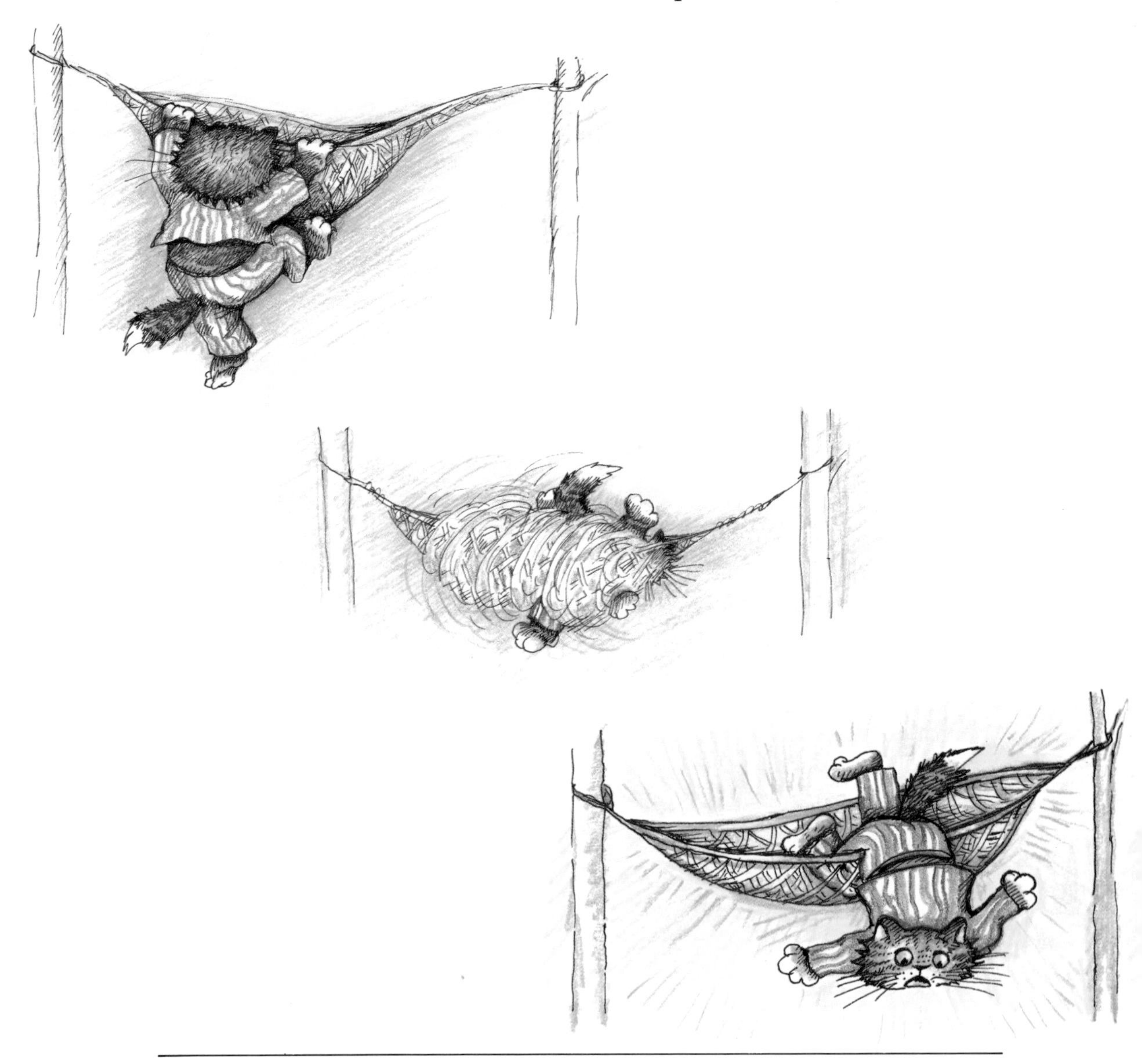

It was a fine morning when she awoke. She ran to the window and looked out. What a marvellous view she had from the tree house.

All around her tall trees reached to the sky. Brightly coloured birds and butterflies were flying everywhere, and the warm air was filled with the perfume of flowers.

The forest was truly magical.

A little green tree frog climbed up to the tree house and dropped in to meet Maisie. His name was Fernando. A big red parrot called Pedro flew in to speak to her.
"Hello Maisie! Scottie Kittie!"

Daddy made a swing for Maisie and hung it from the branch of a tree. They all went out to watch her trying it out. She really enjoyed making new friends on her first day in the forest! That night she telephoned Granny on Daddy's portable phone to tell her she had arrived safely. She told granny about meeting Mr Catnipp, and Pedro and Fernando, and all about the tree house and her swing.

"I hope you are remembering to wear your vest," said Granny. "Please take care of yourself, now."

"I will, Granny. Daddy says I must stay beside him, *and* I've promised not to speak to any snakes or crocodiles. Don't worry. I'm having a lovely holiday."

"SNAKES AND CROCODILES!!" gasped Granny as she put down the phone. "Well, it isn't MY idea of a lovely holiday. Dearie me, my poor wee Maisie." But Maisie was having the time of her life!

Fernando the frog took her fishing on a little lake nearby, where it was safe for kittens. Maisie caught three big fish, and cooked them for tea!

Sometimes it was very rainy in the rainforest, and Pedro the parrot sheltered in the tree house, and played with Maisie. She taught him songs and how to dance the Highland Fling, and he taught Maisie how to dance the Samba, like the cats in RIO.

"Do you know any Scottie birdies?" asked Pedro.

"Oh yes," said Maisie. "Mrs McKitty has a budgie called Billy. He can talk Pan Loaf! . . . and Miss Gingersnapp has a little yellow bird who sings songs to me. He's called Sean Canary, after a famous film star!"

Daddy's friend, Toocooroocoo, took them on an expedition deep into the heart of the forest where he lived with his tribe of spotty cats. It was very exciting! Every night they camped under the stars, and every morning Maisie had to empty hundreds of creepy-crawlies and long-legged beasties out of her wellies!

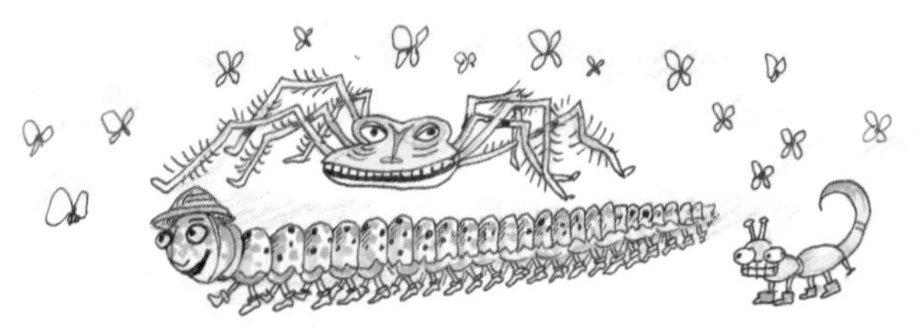

Toocooroocoo showed them a valley where there were golden yellow monkeys in the trees, and frogs which could fly.
He brought them nuts and wild honey and sweet green bananas. Maisie ate too many bananas and turned green too, but Toocooroocoo knew where to find a medicine plant to make her better. The forest was full of surprises!

I Left my heart in Auchtermuchty

Maisie and Daddy thanked Toocooroocoo for being their guide. "I've had a lovely holiday." Maisie told him. "I really like being in the forest --- I even like the creepy-crawlies! You are so lucky to live in such a beautiful place."

Toocooroocoo looked sad.

"We think so too, Maisie, but soon it may all be gone forever." Maisie suddenly remembered what Daddy had written to her about the forest disappearing.

"But how can that be? Is it by magic? Will the forest come back again?"

Toocooroocoo shook his head.

"No. Once it is gone, it can never return. A big company is going to buy the forest and cut down all the trees. They will make lots of money from selling the wood."

Maisie was very upset.

"But what will happen to all the animals, and the birds and flowers? Where will you go? We must *stop* them!"

Daddy took her paw in his.

"We've tried to stop them, Maisie, but it is no use. The company is The Snatchitt Corporation, one of the richest in the world. They don't care about anything except money. Rainforests are not just beautiful places, you see. They are very important. They soak up rain, then give it back to the air when we need it. If they all disappear the weather will go wrong *all over the world*!"

That night, tucked up in her hammock, Maisie tossed and turned trying to think how she could help. There wasn't much time, and she was just a little kitten. This is really a job for Super Cat, she thought. She remembered watching the film on the plane, and her dream, and meeting Mr Catnipp. This gave her an idea!

As soon as she got up in the morning, she made a telephone call. When it was over, she hoped she would soon have a nice surprise for Daddy and Toocooroocoo!

Two days later, Maisie and Daddy were busy having breakfast in their tree house, when they heard a loud whirring noise in the sky above them. Pedro flew down from his tree, flapping his wings.

''NOISY BIRDIE! NOISY BIRDIE!'' he squawked.

There was something in the sky, above the clouds, but Daddy couldn't make it out.

''Is it a bird? Is it a plane?'' he asked Maisie.

''Maybe it's *SUPER CAT*!'' cried Maisie.

They climbed down the ladder and ran out to see what it could be. As the noise grew louder, Toocooroocoo and the spotted cats came out of the rainforest to look too.

At last, when it was right above their heads, they saw that it was a red helicopter!

Daddy was amazed when he saw what was written on its side . . . *S.C.*!

Could it *really* be Super Cat? Had he come to the rescue?

When the helicopter landed, Daddy held his breath!

Out jumped a stripey cat in a yellow shirt. He didn't look a bit like Super Cat. Daddy couldn't help feeling disappointed, but Maisie rushed to meet the stranger, looking very happy. Who could he be?

The stripey cat came towards Daddy and shook his paw.

"Dr Mackenzie, I presume," he said with a smile. "I'm Stanley Catnipp, and I'm very pleased to to meet you. Maisie and I met on the plane to Rio and became good friends. She telephoned me on Tuesday and told me all about the rainforest, and I think I have some good news for you all! I may not be Super Cat, but thanks to Maisie, I've been able to help the world. *I've* bought the

forest, but I've come to hand it over to Toocooroocoo and his tribe. It will belong to them forever!''

''WHOOPEE!'' cried Maisie. ''*Thank you*, Mr S.C.!''

Daddy and Toocooroocoo jumped for joy! Toocooroocoo said he would show Mr Catnipp all the medicine plants in the forest, and maybe his tribe could help to do some good for the world. The wonderful news soon spread everywhere, and all the spotty cats came running to join in saying Thank You. Maisie rushed off to phone Granny and tell her all about it.

''What a happy ending!'' cried Granny. ''I hope you will invite your friend to come home with you and Daddy. Mrs McKitty says she will bake a special cake, and polish her silver teapot!''

Toocooroocoo gave a big feast to celebrate the good news. All the birds and animals came out to watch as Maisie, dressed up in her best party frock, led everyone in a samba dance through the forest! It was a day none of them would ever forget --- the day the rainforest was saved.

S.C.

Maisie's friends in the rainforest never forgot the time she came to visit them. Every day Pedro the parrot sang to them the songs Maisie had taught him.

O, ye canny shove yer Granny off a bus,
Ye canny shove yer Granny off a bus,
Ye canny shove yer Granny, for she's yer Mammy's Mammy,
O, ye canny shove yer Granny off a bus.

Ye can shove yer other Granny off a bus,
Ye can shove yer other Granny off a bus,
Ye can shove yer other Granny, for she's yer Daddy's Mammy,
But ye canny shove yer Granny off a bus.

If you like playing football, clap your paws,
If you like playing football, clap your paws,
For there is no game that's greater,
From Leith Walk to the Equator,
So if you like playing football, clap your paws!

If you like playing football, clap your paws,
If you like playing football, clap your paws,
For there is no game that's finer,
From Dundee to Carolina,
So if you like playing football, clap your paws!

I left my heart in Auchtermuchty,
I left my legs in Timbuktu,
I left my knees in Mississippi, and my paws in Auchenshoogle,
But what is left belongs to you!

Glossary

tattie scone	endearment— (potato scone)
Pan Loaf	Morningside accent— an affected way of speaking
Och aye, the noo	Scottish expression (oh yes, now!) Literal translation— doesn't mean anything
Auchtermuchty *Auchenshoogle*	Scottish place names
easy-osy	easy going
midgie	gnat, midge